ARCTIC OCEAN

to the North Pole

ST. PETERSBURG, RUSSIA

Europe

BLACK SEA

TURKEY

MEDITERRANEAN SEA

KID CLASSICS

FRANKENSTEIN

THE ILLUSTRATED *Just-for-Kids* EDITION

WRITTEN BY MARY SHELLEY · EDITED BY MARGARET NOVAK · ILLUSTRATED BY MAÏTÉ SCHMITT

"Did I request thee, Maker, from my clay /
To mold me man?"

—*John Milton,* Paradise Lost

How It All Started

The biggest volcano ever recorded by humankind erupted in Indonesia over two hundred years ago, covering all of Europe with ash, fog, and cold rain that lasted for months and months. Because of this strange and eerie weather, people called 1816 "the year without a summer."

That gloomy summer, Mary Shelley and her friends were on vacation in the mountains by Geneva, Switzerland, but they were kept indoors by the dreadfully strange weather.

Obsessed with ghost stories, the friends challenged each other to write a horror story and see whose was best. The party went to bed after midnight, but Mary couldn't decide what to write, and she couldn't sleep. Then, as if in a dream, an enormous creature loomed over her, and she knew that she had the idea for *Frankenstein*.

In her tale, Victor Frankenstein is a young scientist determined to discover the elixir of life. He figures it out and uses it to turn dead body parts into a giant, supersmart, super-strong superhuman. The problem is that his creation looks like a scary monster!

And the monster isn't too happy about being a monster, either. All he wants is friendship, and maybe even love. But everyone he meets is terrified of him. He wonders, why did Victor Frankenstein make him, only for him to be so hated? He vows to seek revenge on his creator, and trouble ensues.

This is a shortened, just-for-kids version of Mary Shelley's classic novel. When you are ready, you must read the original—if you dare!

Dear reader,

I am writing this in case you never hear from me again.
Something very strange has happened!

Our ship was stuck in the ice and surrounded by fog
somewhere near the North Pole. When the fog lifted,
we saw a dogsled whizzing across a glacier. The
dogsled was driven by what I can only describe as a
monster. We watched him with our telescopes until he
disappeared. It's impossible for anyone to live this far
north, so we wondered: How on earth he could be here?

The next morning, when I went up on deck, the sailors
were talking to someone in the sea. It was a young
man sitting on a chunk of ice that was drifting in the
ocean. He said his name was Dr. Victor Frankenstein,
and he was nearly frozen to death. We helped him up
and wrapped him in blankets.

When I asked Dr. Frankenstein why he was so far north, he said that he was chasing the monster whom we had seen dogsledding over the glacier. I asked him why, and Dr. Frankenstein said that the story was unbelievable, and that it had ruined his life. But he hoped that we could learn from his mistakes. Then he began his strange and horrifying tale, which I have written down here, in this book.

—Arctic explorer and adventurer, Robert Walton

Chapter 1

My name is Victor Frankenstein. I was born in Naples, Italy, and I grew up in Geneva, Switzerland. Before I start this story, I must tell you about something that happened when I was four years old.

My father's good friend died, and a few months later, he received a letter from her husband, asking my father to take care of their baby, Elizabeth. "It is my wish," the letter said, "that you treat her as your own daughter."

My father went to Italy to bring little Elizabeth Lavenza back to her new home. My mother said that she was the most beautiful child she had ever seen, so gentle and loving. Elizabeth became my friend. She was sweet, imaginative, and playful. Everyone adored Elizabeth.

My brothers were much younger than me, so I felt lucky to have Elizabeth and a friend my age from school: Henry Clerval. Henry was always reading, composing songs, and writing tales of enchantment and knightly adventure.

My childhood was so happy. My parents gave us anything we wanted, and my friends were kind. School was fun, even the hard classes.

I enjoy thinking about my childhood, before bad luck came and changed my hopes into gloomy thoughts.

Science has guided my fate. When I was thirteen years old, we were on vacation, and bad weather forced us to stay inside an inn the whole time. There, I found a dusty old book filled with the peculiar ideas of Cornelius Agrippa, a scientist and alchemist who was obsessed with dark magic. I loved it, but my father said, "Oh, my dear Victor, do not waste your time on this. It is trash."

If he had explained to me that this ancient alchemist had been proven wrong, and that modern science had replaced his mystical ideas, I would have studied modern chemistry instead. Maybe then my ideas would never have led to my ruin.

When I got back home, I read every book I could find by this author, and then other ancient dark magic scientists as well. I told Elizabeth about my discoveries, but she wasn't interested, so I studied alone.

I dreamed of discovering the elixir of life, a potion that cures all diseases and makes you immortal. I became obsessed with it! What if I could cure all sicknesses and make everyone immune to death?

Nature fascinated me. When I was about fifteen years old, I saw a terrible thunderstorm, and watched it with curiosity and delight. I saw a stream of fire flash through an old oak tree, and as soon as the dazzling light vanished, the oak had disappeared. Nothing remained but a blasted stump. I'd never seen anything so destroyed.

When I asked my father where thunder and lightning come from, he said "electricity" and described its power. To show me how it worked, he made a kite that drew sparks of lightning from the clouds. That was when I knew that I wanted to be a scientist when I grew up.

Chapter 2

When I turned seventeen, my parents decided that I should go to college at the University of Ingolstadt in Germany. But before the day to leave arrived, the first misfortune of my life occurred.

Elizabeth caught scarlet fever—a dangerous disease—but she quickly recovered. We urged my mother to stay away from her. At first, Mama listened, but when she heard that Elizabeth was recovering, she entered her room before the danger of infection was over. Three days later, my mother got sick, and her fever was very bad.

When she died, she held our hands and said, "I'm sorry that I am taken from you. Still, I hope to meet you in another world."

I cannot describe how sad and empty we felt. It was a long time before I really believed that she was gone forever, and that the sound of her sweet, familiar voice would never be heard again. She was dead, but we had to live on.

The day of my departure for college arrived, and Henry spent the last evening with us. He was sad that he couldn't come with me. His father wanted him to become a business partner instead. When I left early the next morning, tears flowed from Elizabeth's eyes.

As I left, I became sad. I had always been surrounded by good friends, but now I was alone. At college, I would have to make new friends, and I worried that no one would like me. Still, I wanted to learn. I wanted to take my place in the world.

Chapter 3

I arrived at college and the next morning, I went to see Mr. Krempe, who taught science. He was polite and asked me questions about what I liked to study. I mentioned the ancient alchemy books I had read.

The professor said, "Have you really spent your time studying such nonsense?"

I said yes.

"Every minute," he continued, "that you have wasted on those books is entirely lost. No one told you that those books are a thousand years old?! You must begin your studies all over again."

He wrote down a list of books for me to get, after mentioning that next week he would be teaching science and that Mr. Waldman would be teaching chemistry.

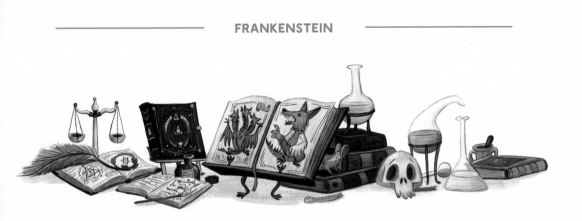

I went home, but I didn't feel like studying. I didn't like modern science. It was different back when the ancient mystical scientists searched for immortality and power. Now a good student was supposed to ignore all the magical things I liked most.

Partly from curiosity, and partly from boredom, I went to Mr. Waldman's class. He seemed kind. He began his class with a history of chemistry. He ended by saying something I would never forget: "The ancient teachers of this science," he said, "promised impossibilities, and made nothing. Today's scientists promise little but have made miracles. They investigate the hidden parts of nature and show how she works. They have new and almost unlimited powers."

I left happy with Mr. Waldman and his class. I paid him a visit the same evening. He welcomed me into his house. He smiled when I told him about the ancient alchemy books I had read. He said, "Modern scientists owe them a debt for their knowledge. The works of geniuses, even if wrong, are almost always good for humanity." I told him that his class had made me more curious about modern chemists, and I asked him what books I should read.

"I would be a very bad chemist if I only studied chemistry," said Mr. Waldman. "If you want to become a true scientist, you should study every book you can get your hands on."

He took me into his lab and showed me the scientific machines. He promised that I could use them when I knew enough not to break anything.

That was an important day for me. In fact, it decided my future.

Chapter 4

From that day, I was obsessed with chemistry. I read books, I attended classes, and I made friends with other chemistry students. Mr. Waldman became my friend. He made things easy to understand. Soon, I worked all night in the lab.

I worked so hard that I amazed my teachers. This went on for two years, and during that time, I didn't go back home. At the end of those two years, I was ready to see my family, but something happened that made me stay.

I was curious about where life came from, so I decided to study the body. I needed to understand how things die and decay. I was not superstitious, but I needed to truly understand life and how it led to death. I spent days and nights in morgues and the university's cadaver lab. And then I learned something astonishing. After weeks of working and being very tired, I discovered how life begins and how to bring something dead back to life!

I was proud of my work. I had learned something that the wisest scientists had tried to discover in the past and failed.

I'm sure that you, reader, would like to know about this secret, but I cannot tell you. Listen patiently until the end of my story, and you will understand why I must never tell you. Learn from me how dangerous some knowledge can be.

I knew I could give life to something as complex and wonderful as a human. I knew I might fail, but I had to try. I decided to make the being very large, a giant, about eight feet tall. After spending a few months collecting tools and materials, I began to work.

It was so exciting! I cared about nothing else. I wanted to create a new species, one which would thank me for giving it life.

From morgues and the cadaver lab, I collected bones, muscle, fat, and other body parts. I worked in a small room at the top of my house. Sometimes, I was disgusted with myself for what I was doing, but I kept at it anyway.

I forgot about my friends and family; I couldn't even think of them until I had succeeded. Now I realize that if you work for something so hard that it makes you forget about friends, family, and the simple pleasures of life, you need to stop.

Winter, spring, and summer went by as I worked, but I didn't even notice, because I was so deeply devoted to my work. I was nervous and feverish. I was worried about the sleepless wreck I had become. Only my enthusiasm kept me going.

Chapter 5

It was on a dreary November night that I finally succeeded. Feeling terribly anxious, I collected the machines around me that would give a spark to the lifeless thing that lay in my room. It was one o'clock in the morning, it was raining, and my candle was nearly burnt out when, by the glimmer of the light, I saw one of the creature's dull yellow eyes open! It breathed hard and moved its arms and legs.

How can I describe how I felt? His body parts were the right size, and I'd made sure that his features were beautiful. His hair was black and flowing; his teeth were white. But his yellow skin barely covered the muscles. And that only looked worse with his watery eyes, his shriveled face, and his weirdly straight black lips.

I'd worked hard for nearly two years to give life to this creature. I was sick and tired. I wanted it so much, but now that I was done, the beauty of that dream vanished, and horror and disgust filled my heart. I couldn't stand what I had created, and I rushed out of the room.

I hid in my bedroom for hours. Then I slept a little, and I had a nightmare. In my dream, I saw Elizabeth, in good health. I embraced her, but as I kissed her, her lips turned to the color of death, and she began to look like the corpse of my dead mother. I woke up in horror; my teeth chattered, and I shook. By the dim light of the moon, I saw the creature—the miserable monster I had created. He loomed over me. His jaws opened, and he made some strange sounds. A crooked grin wrinkled his cheeks.

He held out one hand as if to say hello, but I ran downstairs. I hid in the courtyard for the rest of the night, listening for the thing I had so miserably given life.

No one would believe this horror. A mummy raised from the dead could not be so hideous! I passed the night wretchedly, and my heartbeat was wild. Mingled with fear, I felt the bitterness of disappointment; my dreams had become nightmares!

A rainy morning came, and I saw that it was six o'clock. I walked aimlessly in the streets, afraid that at every turn, I would see the creature. I didn't dare return to my apartment.

I walked for a long time, feeling sick and scared, not daring to look around me. I came to the inn at which carriages usually stopped. Here I saw a horse-drawn carriage coming toward me. It stopped where I was standing, and when the door opened, Henry Clerval jumped out and said, "My dear Frankenstein, how glad I am to see you! How lucky that you should be here right now!"

I was surprised and delighted to see him. I shook his hand and forgot my horror and misfortune. We walked back toward my college, where he told me that he too had begun to study. I asked about my family.

"They are very well, and happy, only worried that they never hear from you," he answered. "By the way," he continued, "you look very ill, so thin and pale."

"You're right," I said, "I've been working hard on one thing and haven't taken enough time to rest, but I hope all that work is over and now I can."

I couldn't tell him about what had happened that night.

Soon, we arrived at my place. I worried that the creature might still be upstairs, walking around. I couldn't let Henry see him! So I asked him to stay at the bottom of the stairs for a few minutes, while I ran up to my room. I shivered in fear as I opened the door, but the apartment was empty. I ran back down the stairs.

We went to my room, but I was unable to contain myself. I trembled, and my heart beat rapidly. I couldn't sit still; I jumped over the chairs, clapped my hands, and laughed out loud. Henry at first thought I was just glad to see him, but my behavior soon frightened him.

"My dear Victor, what is the matter? Why are you laughing like that? You must be sick! What is the cause of all this?"

"Don't ask!" I answered covering my eyes. "Oh, save me!" I imagined that the monster seized me; I fell down in a fit. My poor friend! What must he have thought?

This was the start of a nervous fever, which lasted for several months. During all that time, Henry took care of me. Later, I learned that my father was too ill to come to see me.

But I was also very ill, and only Henry could help me. The monster was always on my mind, and I talked constantly about him. I'm sure my words surprised Henry: he probably thought it was my imagination, but because I kept talking about it, he soon believed that something terrible had happened.

Slowly, I got better. By then, it was already spring, which helped me to feel better. I was still afraid that Henry was going to ask about the monster, but instead he told me that my father and Elizabeth would dearly love to hear from me, and that I should write to them. Of course, I would be happy to! Then he told me that Elizabeth had written me a letter.

Chapter 6

My dearest Victor,

You have been very ill, and Henry's letters have not made me worry less. I have convinced your father not to travel to see you, since it might be dangerous for him. But now, Henry tells me you are getting better, and I hope that you can write soon. We are happy here, and we love you dearly. Please come home when you can; your father is better now and wants to see you.

Do you remember Justine Moritz? She was treated badly by her mother, and now lives with us. Your brother, little William, is growing so tall! I'm feeling better just by writing to you. Please write soon, dear Victor!

Elizabeth

Of course, I wrote back as soon as I read her letter! I started to feel a little better, and in a fortnight I was able to get out of bed and walk around the house.

Then I saw the scientific equipment I had used to make the monster, and it made me feel sick. Henry saw how upset I was, but he never asked what was wrong; he never tried to pry my secret out of me.

In May, I felt strong enough to plan a trip home. Henry suggested that, before leaving, we take a good walk around the city and surrounding country where I had lived these past years. I was happy to do so.

It was a glorious Sunday afternoon. People were dancing, and everyone we met appeared happy. My own spirits were high, and I bounded along with feelings of unbridled joy and hilarity.

Chapter 7

When we got back, I found this letter from my father:

My dear Victor,

I have terrible news for you. Your brother William is dead! That sweet child, who was so gentle . . . Victor, he was murdered!

Last Thursday, Elizabeth, your two brothers, and I went for a walk at a park. The evening was warm, and our walk was longer than usual. It was already dusk before we decided to head home; and then we discovered that William and Ernest, who had gone on before, were not to be found. Ernest came back and asked if we had seen his brother. He said that they'd been playing hide-and-seek, and that William had run away to hide, but Ernest couldn't find him.

We searched for him until night fell, when Elizabeth suggested that he might have returned to the house, but he wasn't there. We searched again with torches. About five in the morning, I discovered my lovely boy, motionless on the grass: the print of the murderer's finger was on his neck.

Elizabeth was in anguish, as we all were. She fainted, and later blamed herself. William had teased her to let him wear a very valuable miniature portrait that she possessed of your mother. This picture is gone, and was doubtless the temptation that urged the murderer to the deed.

Please come home, Victor, and console Elizabeth; she weeps constantly. We are all unhappy, but we would be glad to see you.

Your affectionate father,
Alphonse Frankenstein

I threw the letter on the table, and I covered my face with my hands.

"My dear friend, what has happened?" exclaimed Henry, when he saw me cry.

I told him to read the letter. He did, and tears also came to his eyes.

"I am so sorry, my friend. What do you intend to do?"

"I can't wait another minute. I must go instantly to Geneva to see my family," I answered. "Come with me, Henry, to order the horses."

Henry tried to cheer me up, but it didn't help. We hurried through the streets, and when we reached the horse-drawn carriage, I said goodbye.

My journey was sad. At first, I wished to get home quickly, but when I drew near Geneva, I didn't want to be there. Everything seemed different now, and grief and fear again overcame me. Night had fallen, and when I could hardly see anything, I felt even gloomier. But things would only get worse.

It was completely dark when got to Geneva, and the gates of the town were already shut. I had to pass the night at a village outside the city. I was unable to rest, so I decided to visit the spot where my poor William had died. A storm appeared, and I soon felt the rain coming down in large drops, while thunder rumbled over my head.

As I watched the storm, so terrifying yet beautiful, I yelled, "William! This is your funeral!" As I said these words, I saw in the gloom a figure creeping around behind a clump of trees. I looked closely: I could not be mistaken. A flash of lightning lit up the object, and I saw its shape plainly: its huge size, its hideous body, and instantly I knew that it was him, the filthy creature I had made.

Why was he there? Could he be my brother's murderer? As soon as I had this idea, I was sure it was true. My teeth chattered, and I had to lean against a tree for support. He ran away quickly. I thought about chasing him, but that would have been pointless, for another lighting flash showed him quickly climbing a hill to the south. He reached the top and disappeared.

The thunder stopped, but the rain continued, and the night became completely dark. Almost two years had now passed since the night I gave him life; was this his first crime? I had turned loose a horrible monster on the world, who liked hurting people and causing misery!

No one can imagine the anguish I suffered for the rest of the night, which I spent, cold and wet, outside. But my imagination was busy making up evil scenes.

Day dawned, and I went back to Geneva. The city gates were open, and I hurried to my father's house. My first thought was to tell what I knew of the murderer. But I stopped when I thought about saying that I had created a monster and brought it to life. I knew that if anyone else told such a story to me, it would have seemed crazy. Besides, how could they catch him, even if they believed me? So, I said nothing.

I got to my father's house at about five in the morning. I went into the library and waited for everyone to get up.

While I was looking at pictures of my mother and my brother William by the fireplace, my brother Ernest entered.

He was glad to see me, but he started to cry. I tried to calm him and asked about our father and Elizabeth. He told me she was the saddest of all, especially since the murderer had been discovered.

"The murderer discovered!" I exclaimed. "How could that be? Who would have tried to chase him? It's impossible. I saw him too; he was free last night!"

"I don't know what you mean," my brother said, "No one would believe it at first, and even now, Elizabeth is not convinced. Who could imagine that Justine Moritz, who was so fond of the family, could suddenly become capable of such a terrible crime?"

"Justine Moritz!" I said. "That's not true, everyone knows that; no one believes it, surely?"

"No one did at first, but we have learned several things, and her own behavior has been strange, which adds to the evidence and leaves no hope for doubt. She will go on trial today, and then you will hear all of it."

He told me that the morning when poor William had been discovered, Justine was sick, and stayed in her bed for several days after that. During this time, someone was washing the clothes Justine had worn on the night of the murder, and discovered in her pocket the precious portrait of my mother. Justine must have stolen it! She was arrested. When she was accused of theft and murder, the poor girl confirmed everyone's suspicions by her confusing behavior.

This was a strange story, but it did not prove to me that she was guilty, and I replied, "You are all mistaken; I know the murderer. Justine—poor, good Justine—is innocent."

Just then, my father entered. He looked unhappy, but he tried to welcome me cheerfully. Then Ernest exclaimed, "Papa! Victor says that he knows who killed poor William."

"We also do, unfortunately," replied my father. "I would rather have never known, than have learned of such evil in one I liked so much."

"Papa, you are mistaken," I said. "Justine is innocent."

"If she is, I hope she does not suffer. She is to be tried today, and I hope that she will be set free."

I was convinced that Justine was innocent. But I couldn't tell anyone what I knew. Would anyone believe that I had let loose such a monster on the world?

We were soon joined by Elizabeth, who was happy to see me.

"You being here fills me with hope," she said. "Perhaps you can show that Justine is innocent? If she is condemned, I will never be happy again."

"She is innocent," I said, "and that shall be proved."

"How kind and generous you are," she said. "Everyone else thinks she's guilty, and that makes me sad, because I know it's impossible." She wept.

"Dry your tears, my dear," my father said. "If she is innocent, trust in our laws."

Chapter 8

The trial started at eleven o'clock, and I went with my family to court. I knew that I had created the murderous monster and that Justine was innocent, but who would believe me? I would sound crazy!

Justine looked calm and confident of her innocence. She looked sad when she saw us. The trial began, and the charges were read against her. She had been out all night, and in the morning was seen near where the boy was found. When a woman asked her why she was out there, she'd seemed confused and answered strangely. When she got home and was asked where she'd been, she answered that she'd been out looking for William. She had a fit when she saw that he was dead and stayed in bed for days. It was then that the picture he'd worn was found in her clothes.

Justine was called on for her defense. She now seemed surprised, horrified, and miserable. She insisted that she was completely innocent.

She said that on that night, she'd visited an aunt in a nearby village. When she returned and was told of the missing boy, she went looking for him. By then, the city gates were shut, and she spent the night in a barn. She thought she heard some footsteps early in the morning and went out at dawn to look again. She couldn't explain how she had my mother's picture and thought that the murderer might have placed it in her skirt pocket while she slept.

Elizabeth defended her, saying that she'd known Justine for years. She spoke of Justine's kindness to my family, and her fondness for William, acting almost like a mother to him. There was no reason for her to do something so terrible, Elizabeth said.

It didn't seem to be enough to convince everyone that Justine was innocent. I was nervous and upset during the whole trial. I knew she was innocent; could my creation have been so evil as to kill the boy and then to make it look like she had done it? I worried that the court had already decided that Justine was guilty. I felt terrible and so guilty for what I had done.

That night I hardly slept, and in the morning, I went back to the court, fearing the worst. An officer told me what I most feared: Justine had been found guilty.

Words cannot tell you the sadness I experienced in that moment. And even worse, Justine had confessed to the crime.

This was strange and unexpected; what could it mean? Had my eyes deceived me? I hurried home, and Elizabeth wanted to know what they had decided. I told her that the judges had ruled against her, and that she had also confessed. This was terrible news for poor Elizabeth.

"How will I ever again believe in human goodness?" she cried. "Justine, whom I loved like a sister, how could she pretend to be innocent, and then betray us?"

Soon after, we heard that Justine wanted to see Elizabeth. Elizabeth agreed to go, as long as I went with her.

We entered the gloomy prison cell and saw Justine sitting on some straw; her hands were cuffed, and her head rested on her knees. She rose when she saw us, and threw herself at Elizabeth's feet, weeping bitterly.

"Oh, Justine!" said Elizabeth, "Why did you take away my last hope? I relied on your innocence, and I am so miserable now."

Justine cried too, sad that Elizabeth would think she was guilty. Elizabeth still wanted to believe her innocent, unless she admitted to the murder right there.

Justine admitted that she had lied when she confessed. She had been pressured to confess and was told that she would be condemned forever if she did not. She felt terrible that Elizabeth could think her capable of committing such an awful crime.

"Oh, Justine!" Elizabeth exclaimed. "Forgive me for not trusting you. But do not fear; I will prove your innocence, and you will not be executed."

Justine shook her head sadly, and said that she already accepted her fate, whatever it might be.

Justine came to me, and said she hoped I didn't think she was guilty. My voice caught in my throat and I couldn't answer her, but Elizabeth told her that I did not. Justine was grateful for that.

But I knew that I had created the true murderer, and nothing could make me feel better.

We stayed several hours with Justine, and it was with great difficulty that Elizabeth could tear herself away. "I wish," she cried, "that I were to die with you; I cannot live in this world of misery."

Justine tried to be cheerful, and she fought back her bitter tears. She embraced Elizabeth and said, kindly, "Farewell, my dearest friend, and may this be the last sorrow you ever suffer. Live, and be happy, and make others so."

Elizabeth tried to convince the authorities of Justine's innocence, but she failed, and Justine was executed the following day. I tried to appeal to them, but they wouldn't listen to me either.

This was all my fault! William and Justine were the first victims of my terrible work.

Chapter 9

Justine was gone, and I was still alive. I had wanted to do good in the world, but now everything had gone wrong. I was so remorseful and guilty; I can hardly describe it.

I got sick again and avoided people; I just wanted to be alone. My father saw my pain and tried to comfort me, telling me that he was sad for William as well, but saying that if we stayed that way for too long, we would never be happy again, or even be able to live normal lives. This was good advice, but still, I tried to avoid seeing him.

About this time, we went to our vacation house in Bellerive, Switzerland, which was good for me. Often, after everyone else had gone to bed, I took the boat, and spent many hours on the water.

At these times, I cried and wished that I could be at peace again. But I had created something horrible, and I lived in daily fear that the monster might do some new evil. I wanted revenge for William and Justine.

My father's health was now worse because of the horror of the recent events. Elizabeth was sad and no longer enjoyed her daily life. She told me that after Justine was gone, she no longer could see the world the way she had before. We both knew that Justine was innocent. And I knew the true murderer was still free.

Elizabeth saw my anguish and tried to comfort me, but even her kindness could not make me feel better. So, I decided to go away to a nearby valley that I had enjoyed as a boy. I took a mule and walked into the mountains. It was summer, nearly two months after Justine was taken from us. The weather was good, and as I climbed higher I began to feel better. The beautiful scenery lifted my spirits.

I admired the great mountains and found a place to stay in a little village. There, I finally gave in to sleep, and welcomed it.

Chapter 10

The next day, I explored the valley and again saw the beauty of that place: snowy mountaintops, pine forests, soaring eagles. All of it made me begin to feel better.

Rain came, but I decided to climb a nearby mountain anyway with only my mule. It was tough and even dangerous, but the scenery was so amazing, and I wondered if we as humans were really as superior as we thought we were.

It was nearly noon when I arrived at the top, where I sat for a while. A mist covered the mountains all around me. Then a breeze blew away the clouds, and I climbed down to an ice glacier. The surface was uneven, rising like the waves of the sea.

As I looked out at the surrounding mountains, I suddenly saw a figure in the distance, coming toward me. He bounded over the ice, and he was taller than a normal man. I knew that it was the monster! I trembled with rage, deciding to wait and fight him. As he approached, he looked miserable, and his unearthly ugliness made his face almost too horrible for human eyes. But I barely even saw how he looked, because I was so angry.

"How dare you approach me?" I demanded. "Don't you fear my vengeance? Go away, vile insect! Or stay, so I can pound you to dust! I wish I could bring back those you have taken!"

"I expected this response," he said. "How I am hated, I who am miserable beyond all living things! Even you, my creator, detest and reject me, your own creature. We are bound together, and we will be until one of us is gone. You wish to kill me. But if you will agree to my conditions, I will leave you in peace. And if you refuse, I will take away your remaining friends."

"Monster! You are a fiend! Torture is too good for you! Come here, so I can extinguish the spark of life that I never should have given you."

My rage was endless; I sprang at him, feeling courage in that moment.

He easily stepped to one side and said: "Be calm! I ask you to listen to me, before you give in to your hatred. Have I not suffered enough, that you wish to increase my misery? Life is dear to me, and I will defend it. Remember, you made me more powerful than you. I am taller and stronger, but I will not fight you; I am your creation and will obey you, if you will accept me. Everywhere I see happiness, but I cannot take part in it. Make me happy again, and I will be good."

"Go away!" I said, "I will not listen. There can be no friendship between you and me; we are enemies. Leave or we must fight, and one must fall."

"How can I convince you? " said the monster. "Will nothing make you look on me kindly? Believe me, Frankenstein: I was good; my soul glowed with love and humanity, but I am miserably alone. If you hate me; what hope can I have from your fellow humans? I hide up here; I live in ice caves. The stormy skies are kinder to me than humanity. If people knew of my existence, they would do as you do, and wish for my destruction. Shall I not hate them who hate me? But you have the power to help me. Take the time to listen to me, then do what you wish. But hear me, Frankenstein. You accuse me of murder. I don't ask you to spare me, just listen to me. Then, if you wish, destroy your work."

"I curse the day I made you!" I yelled. "Get out of my sight!"

"I will leave you. But hear my tale; it is long and strange, and it is cold out here. Come to my hut on the mountain. By the time the sun sets, you will know my story. You can choose if I leave the world behind and lead a harmless life, or become the enemy of humanity, and the cause of your own ruin."

He led the way across the ice, and I followed. I didn't answer him, but as I walked, I thought about his words and decided to listen to his tale. I was curious now. Before, I only wanted to know if he had murdered my brother William. Now I felt that I should listen before I judged him. We crossed the ice and climbed the rock. We got to his hut, and, as I seated myself by the fire he'd made, he began his story.

Chapter 11

"It's hard for me to remember my beginning," the monster said. "The light was bright and hurt my eyes, but I could move, and I found myself in a forest near the city. I ate some berries and then fell asleep. When I woke up, I was cold, and it was dark.

"I remember the sunrise, which I enjoyed, but I was also hungry and thirsty. Several days passed, and I learned about animals and plants.

"One day, when I was terribly cold, I found a fire that had been left by some travelers. I was overcome with delight at the warmth. In my joy I thrust my hand into the live embers, but quickly drew it out again with a cry of pain. How strange, I thought, that the same cause should produce such opposite effects! I examined the materials of the fire, and found it to be made of wood. I gathered more branches and roasted roots and nuts, but it was hard to find enough to eat. I knew I had to leave the forest, and after a few days, I came to a big, open field.

"I saw a small hut. The door was open, and I entered. An old man sat near a fire, making his breakfast. He saw me, yelled loudly, and ran away across the fields. I liked the hut: here the snow and rain could not touch me, and the ground was dry. I ate his breakfast and then I was tired, so I went to sleep for a while. I woke up later and left.

"Soon, I arrived at a village. It looked wonderful! I admired the cottages and houses. I saw the gardens, and milk and cheese placed at a kitchen window, which made me hungry again. I went into one cottage, but the children inside shrieked, and one of the women fainted. The whole village was frightened; some even attacked me.

"I escaped to the country and hid in a boarded-up shed. It was built against the back of a larger cottage and surrounded by a pig sty. It kept out the snow and rain, and it was cozy enough for me.

"I decided to stay there for a while, and soon, I saw a girl with a bucket outside, passing by. Her hair was braided, and she looked patient yet sad. I discovered that I could see the inside the cottage by spying through the wall.

"In one corner near a small fire sat an old man. Soon, the same girl sat down beside the old man, who picked up an instrument and began to play; he made such beautiful music! It was so lovely; it made her cry. They were so kind to each other that I had to stop watching; it was too emotional for me. A sad-eyed young man returned to the cottage with wood. All three of them sat down to eat a meal. After that, they lit the cottage with candles, and the young man read aloud from a book before they went to bed."

Chapter 12

The monster continued, "I couldn't sleep. I kept thinking about these people, and how gentle they were. I wanted to join them, but I didn't dare, because I remembered how the villagers had treated me.

"I watched them for days. The young man and woman seemed unhappy, and I learned it was because they were poor. They were often hungry, and they gave up their food for the old man, who was blind. They kept none for themselves.

"I decided to help them a little, in secret, and gathered wood to help their fire, leaving it at their door. I remember how amazed the girl was when she opened the door one morning and saw the wood pile!

"By listening, I learned the words, *fire, milk, bread,* and *wood.* I also learned the names of the cottagers themselves. The young man was Felix; the girl was his sister, Agatha; and the old man was their father.

"I spent the winter there, listening to them and watching them. Felix read to his father sometimes. I learned that it was possible to put words on paper, and it made me want to learn to read, too.

"I had admired the looks of these cottagers—their grace, beauty, and charming expressions. So, imagine how I felt when I saw my own reflection in a pool of water. I could not believe it. I realized that I am a monster!

"When it was dark, I went into the woods to gather firewood for them. They were always thankful for it, even though they didn't know where it came from. It pleased me to see them happy.

"I wanted to learn more about them, and I thought, foolishly, that we might be able to be friends," sighed the monster. "I imagined introducing myself to them, thinking that at first, they would be fearful, but would soon see that I was gentle, and so they would like me, maybe even love me."

Chapter 13

"Spring came, and the weather was fine," said the monster.
"One day, someone knocked on the cottage door. It was a lady
on horseback. She was dressed all in black and wore a veil.
Felix ran to her and hugged her. She drew back her veil and
smiled at him. She was beautiful, with black, braided hair.

"She didn't speak their language but was learning it. She
stayed with them, and I discovered that her name was Safie.
She played the guitar very well, and they enjoyed listening
to her. Since they were teaching her, I was able to better learn

the language myself, and I began to understand everything they said.

"I also learned more about the world, as they taught Safie history and geography. I learned that people could be noble and good, but also cruel and evil. I learned about nations and wealth, and how some people were very rich, and some very poor.

"Since I had nothing, I knew I must be poor, and of no real value to others. I was larger and stronger than them, but there was no one else in this world like me. I was a monster.

"This made me so sad. I tried not to think about it, but the more I learned by listening to them, the worse I felt. I admired these people and their goodness, but I knew I could never be a part of it. I could only watch them in secret and listen and learn— and wish that I could have their friendship and love.

"Where were my friends and relations? I had no parents who had looked out for me. What was I? I had no answers."

Chapter 14

The monster continued his tale. "I learned that the old man was called De Lacey, and that he came from Paris, France. His children, Felix and Agatha, had grown up there too.

"Safie's father, whom the De Laceys called the Turk, had been the cause of their downfall. He was from Turkey and had lived in Paris for several years. But at some point, he angered the French government, and was put in prison. He was set to be executed, even though he was innocent.

"Felix was at the trial. He was outraged by the unfair decision and wanted to help the man. Felix found a window at the prison, where the Turk was being held, and spoke to him about how he might escape.

"It was at the Turk's prison cell that Felix met Safie, and the two began to fall in love. She wanted to get married, so Felix developed a plan. The night before the Turk's execution,

Felix helped him escape. He, Safie, and Felix fled France to northern Italy. But the Turk wanted to return to his homeland.

"The Turk was now less happy about Felix and Safie being together, but he was afraid that Felix might turn him in to the Italian police, so he kept quiet. He secretly planned to take his daughter back with him to his own country.

"But then news arrived from Paris. The government had discovered that Felix had freed the Turk, and had arrested De Lacey and Agatha and thrown them in prison. Felix had no choice but to go back and try to beg for them to be released. He made the Turk promise to leave Safie in Italy until he could return. Felix, Agatha, and De Lacey were put in jail for five months, and at their trial, they were told to leave France and never return.

"They found this cottage in Germany, and Felix learned that Safie and the Turk had left Italy. This was why he was so sad when I first saw him.

"But Safie got away. She found a way to sneak out, and, learning where Felix was, she decided to go to him."

Chapter 15

"This was the story of the people in the cottage," said the monster, "and I was impressed by it. I admired them all."

"One night, when I was in the woods, I found a suitcase that had some clothes and books inside. The books were history and literature. I loved them and read them all. They made me wonder, who was I? What was I? Where did I come from? Where was I going? I still haven't answered these questions.

"But I knew that I was different from people, and this made me feel bitter. I also discovered some of your notes, Victor,

hidden in the clothing I'd worn when I left your lab. There were details about how you made me. I learned what I really was, and it disgusted me!

"But I decided that I should reveal myself to the people in the cottage, trusting that they would be kind to me after hearing my story. Still, I was worried they would hate me, so I put it off for many months.

"Autumn came, and I saw how kind they were to others, even the poor who came to their door. Would they turn me away? I worried that they might.

"I realized that if De Lacey could accept me (since he was blind), then the others might, too.

"One day, Safie, Agatha, and Felix went for a walk. De Lacey played his guitar. I was scared, because I was going to talk to him! I went to his front door and knocked.

"He asked me to come in. I told him I was sorry to bother him, and that I was a traveler who wanted to rest for a short time. De Lacey was kind and asked me to stay.

"I told him that I was sad, and all alone. He said not to be sad. I told him that I felt like a monster, and that no one would be my friend, but that there were people nearby whom I wished to be friends with, since they were very kind. He offered to help me and said that he would try to convince them of my goodness. I thanked him.

"He wanted to know the names of these people that I wished to be friends with. I didn't know what to do; this was the moment I was so scared of! But I took his hand and told him that it was him and his excellent family."

"'Who are you?'" he asked.

"Just then, the door opened. Felix, Safie, and Agatha had returned. They saw me, and they were horrified. Felix pulled my hand away from his father. He threw me to the ground and hit me with a stick. I could have fought back and hurt him, but I didn't. Instead, I ran out, back to my hiding place in the shed, where they didn't see me."

Chapter 16

"Oh, I was so miserable! I could have destroyed them and their cottage, but of course, I didn't. When night came, I left and wandered the woods like a wild beast. The stars shone and an owl hooted. The whole world was at peace, except for me."

"I sat down and decided that there was nothing that anyone could do to help me. I knew then that all humans were my enemies, especially you, Victor, the man who had made me! As the sun came up, I heard voices in the distance, and I knew that I couldn't go back to my hiding place, so I hid in the forest.

"As I thought about it, I realized that I might have acted too soon with De Lacey. I should have become good friends with him first, and then he could have introduced me to the others when they were ready. Maybe there was still hope! I decided to go back and try again.

"But when I got back to the cottage, no one was there. So, I hid and waited. Eventually, Felix came back with some friends. I heard him tell them that he and his family had to leave. He said that their family was in great danger by staying there. He went into the cottage for a bit and then left. I never saw him or the others again.

"I stayed in my hiding place for the rest of the day, feeling sad. The people whom I would have been friends with were gone. The more I thought about it, the angrier I became. That night, I snuck out and set the cottage on fire. It burned wildly in the wind, and then I left.

"I'd learned enough about you, Victor, to know that you lived in Geneva, Switzerland, so that's where I headed. I was determined to have justice from you.

"While walking through a deep wood, I saved a young girl from slipping into a river and drowning, but the people she was with didn't thank me. One threw a rock at me!

"That was my reward for saving her! The pain was so bad
that I fainted. Eventually, my wound healed, but my anger
did not go away.

"Finally, I arrived near your home in Geneva. As I hid again
in a forest, a beautiful child came toward me. I thought that
since he was so young, he might be able to be my friend, and
not be scared of me.

"So, I reached out to him, but he screamed and called
me a monster. I told him that I wouldn't hurt him, but
he thought I was going to eat him. He called me an
ugly ogre and demanded that I let him go. He said his
father was Mr. Frankenstein, who would punish me.
Frankenstein! My enemy!

"He kept screaming at me, and I put my hand on his throat to try to quiet him, but in a minute, he was dead. I saw that he was wearing something pretty: a glittering portrait of a woman. I took it.

"I left that spot and looked for a place to hide. I found a barn that seemed to be empty, but I saw a young woman sleeping inside on some straw. I whispered in her ear to wake up.

"She stirred, but didn't wake up, so, feeling wicked, I placed the glittering portrait into her dress pocket, and crept out of the barn. She would take the blame for killing the boy.

"After that, I fled into the mountains. Here I am, alone and miserable, and I will not leave you alone until you can make me a female friend, another monster just like me."

Chapter 17

The monster stopped talking, and looked at me, awaiting my answer. But I was confused, unable to reply.

"You must do this for me," he insisted.

But having heard how he had indeed killed my brother, I was furious. "I refuse," I said. "Nothing you can do to me will make me change my mind. I will never make another monster like you!"

"I will be honest with you," the monster said. "I hurt people because I am sad, and hated by everyone. I would love to live among people and be accepted for who I am, but everyone, even you, wants to destroy me. If I cannot be at peace, I will have my revenge. I will make you fear me and wish you had never been born!"

Then he seemed to calm down. "If anyone would just be kind to me, I would be kind a hundred times more back to them, but it seems this isn't possible. So, if you will make another creature to be with me, that will be enough. We will have each other and will leave people alone. Please, my creator, make me happy! Make me grateful! Have sympathy for me!"

I did feel sorry for him. The idea of making another monster was horrible to me, but I understood his reasons for wanting a friend. I'd made him; how could I deny him this?

"If you do this, you will never see us again," he said. "We will go far away. I see pity in your eyes; do this for me, please!"

"You say you will go away," I answered, "but what if you come back? Then there will be two of you, two who could cause harm. I can't agree to this."

"A moment ago, you felt pity! I promise you: when I have my companion, we will leave the human world and my anger will be gone."

I realized that he spoke the truth. I sympathized with him, and I knew that I had no right to refuse his request.

"Do you promise," I said, "to be gentle? What if you're lying?"

"If I have the love of a friend, I will be happy, I will feel accepted, and won't need anything else."

I thought about all he had said. It wasn't his fault that he was who he was; I had made him that way. So, I said, "I agree, as long as you promise to leave Europe forever, and avoid human company. I will make a friend for you."

"I promise," he cried, "that if you do this, you will never see me again. Go and do your work, and I will wait and watch you. I will be ready when you've finished."

Then he left and went down the mountain. I had spent the whole afternoon with him, and my mind was filled with unhappy thoughts.

The next morning, I returned home. I must have looked terrible, because my family was worried about me. But I could barely speak to them. I knew I had to begin with my horrible work.

Chapter 18

As the days went by, I couldn't start making another monster. I feared that the creature would be angry and take revenge on me, but the thought of making another monster disgusted me. I knew I needed to learn more, but I avoided doing it. At least my health improved again.

One day, my father came to me and said, "I'm happy to see that you are feeling better, my son, but I know that you are still unhappy. So, I have an idea. I have always hoped that you and Elizabeth would get married. But I worry that you aren't interested in her."

"My dear father," I answered, "I assure you that I love her dearly, and hope to marry her one day."

"That makes me happier than I have felt in some time," he said. "Would you be willing to marry her soon? I don't wish to tell you what to do, but our family could use some happiness."

I couldn't answer in that moment. Though I loved Elizabeth, I couldn't marry her right away; I still had my horrible work to do, and a promise to keep. I also knew that I had to go to England and meet with some experts to learn more. Plus, I didn't want to do this horrible task in my father's house! What if something went wrong? What if they discovered what I was doing?

No, once I had finished and the monster was gone, then, and only then, could I agree to marry. So, I told my father that I needed to visit England first, without telling him why. He agreed, because he saw that I was eager to make the journey.

I would be there for a year at most. My father wanted Henry Clerval to go with me. I wanted to be alone, but I was also glad to have a friend.

The only thing that bothered me was that, while I was gone, my family might be attacked by the monster if he changed his mind, or if he thought that I was avoiding my work. Was he watching my every move from the shadows? Would he follow me to England?

I left for England in September. Elizabeth asked me to come back soon, and I was very sad to leave her.

After a few days of travel, I met up with Henry. He seemed so happy, while I was so miserable. We journeyed all the way to Rotterdam, in the Netherlands, and then from there, we took a ship to London, England.

Chapter 19

We stayed in London for several months. It was a wonderful city, and Henry wanted to talk to the many talented geniuses who lived there. But I only wanted to find the knowledge I needed to complete my promise, so I went in search of famous scientists.

At one time, I would have loved to be there, but now, I only gathered information, and didn't have any fun. I always let Henry go out alone. I didn't wish to make friends or even be around others. I collected everything I needed, but I hated it.

We eventually received an invitation to go to Scotland, and I agreed, since I wanted to see mountains again and knew that I could be alone up there and finish my work.

We stopped many places along the way, but I knew that I was not keeping my promise to the monster, and I feared that he might take revenge on my family. I wrote to them and was impatient to hear back, afraid if there was ever any delay in getting an answer by mail. I also worried that he followed me and was nearby, watching me. I was afraid for Henry's safety.

When we reached Scotland, I told Henry that I wished to tour the country on my own. I promised that I would return in a month or two. I wanted to find a remote place to finish my work. I was sure that the monster was watching me.

I went far north, to the Orkney Islands, where only a few villagers lived. I rented a small hut. Its thatched roof was falling in, but it didn't bother me. There, people left me alone.

Even though I had a place and the time, some days I couldn't work at all. But on other days I worked well into the night. When I made the first creature, I was so enthusiastic that I didn't think about how awful it was. But now, I felt sick, knowing what would happen when I finished.

I feared meeting the monster again at any moment, especially when I was alone. Still, I had some hope that when I was finished, I would be free. But the evil of it all horrified me.

Chapter 20

Late one night I wondered whether I should take a break and get some rest. I was almost done making my second monster. But what if she was worse than he was? What if she refused to go with him? What if she didn't like him and abandoned him, as everyone else had done? What if they could have children, and make more monsters?! Would they come back and destroy us all?

I looked out at the moon, and I saw him at the window! A ghastly grin wrinkled his lips as he gazed on me. Yes, he had followed me in my travels; he had crept through forests, hid himself in caves, or taken refuge in empty fields; and he now came to check on my progress and hold me to my promise. As I looked at him, I knew I couldn't go through with it, so I tore the thing in front of me to pieces. He saw me destroy it and howled, and then ran away.

I locked the door. I promised myself that I would never make a monster again, no matter what I'd told him.

After several hours, I heard the sound of a boat and oars near my house.

Then I heard the creaking of my front door, as if someone was trying to open it softly. I trembled from head to toe. I knew who it was, and I wanted to warn the others nearby, but I felt helpless and couldn't move, like when you dream of a danger, but can't get away from it.

I heard footsteps in the hall; my door creaked open, and I saw what I feared most. He entered the room and shut the door, saying, "You have destroyed your work; do you dare to break your promise? I left Switzerland for you. I have been cold and hungry, all to follow you. Do you dare to destroy my hopes?"

"Leave!" I cried. "I do break my promise. I will never create another like you, both monstrous and wicked."

"I reasoned with you before," he said. "But you have proven yourself to be unworthy of my trust. Remember that I have, and I can, make you so miserable that you will hate even daylight. You created me, but you must obey me!"

"You are powerful now," I said, "but your threats do not scare me, or make me want to do more evil. In fact, they prove to me that I was right not to create a wicked friend for you. Leave! Your words will only make me angrier!"

The monster saw how determined I was and gnashed his teeth in anger. "Will every person and animal have a friend except me? Beware! I will have my revenge on you. You will be sorry you've done this to me!"

"Stop!" I yelled. "I have made up my mind and will not change it. Leave me, now!"

"I will go. But remember, I will be with you on your wedding night."

I jumped forward, and I would have grabbed him; but he ran out of the house. In a few moments, I saw him in his boat, which shot swiftly across the water and soon disappeared.

Everything was silent, but his words rung in my ears. I burned with rage to go after him and throw him into the ocean. My imagination thought up a thousand images to worry me.

Why hadn't I followed him? I'd let him leave, and he'd headed toward the mainland. I shuddered to think who his next victim might be. And I remembered his words: "I will be with you on your wedding night." I thought of my beloved Elizabeth, and how horrible it would be for me to be taken from her; I vowed that I would fight him. I slept for a bit, but even then, the monster haunted my dreams.

Later on, I received a letter from Henry. He told me he wanted to travel to India, and how he would get on a train for India in London. He asked me to return to him, so that we could go to London together.

I decided to go back to him, but before I could leave, I had to pack up my equipment from the lab. I gathered my tools. The parts of the creature I would have made were still there, on the floor. I had to get rid of them, so I gathered them together into bags and baskets with heavy stones.

After two o'clock in the morning, I put the bags and baskets in a small boat and sailed far out from shore. There, I cast everything into the sea. It sank, and I sailed away, feeling better. Clouds hid the moon. I fell asleep.

When I woke up, the sun was high in the sky, but I didn't know where I was! There was a strong wind, and I had to sail with it. I didn't have a compass. I feared that my own foolishness would do the monster's work for him. And I worried that I would never see Henry, my father, or Elizabeth again.

After many hours, the wind died, and I saw some land to the south. I saw boats near the shore. I had money with me, and I found a town with a good harbor, which made me relieved. I had landed my boat, and tied it up, when several people came up to me. They seemed worried and whispered to each other. I smiled and asked them the name of the town.

"You will know soon enough," one man answered.

I was surprised at his answer, which seemed rude, and also that the others seemed angry.

"Why do you answer me so roughly?" I asked. "Surely, it is not the custom of the British to receive strangers so rudely."

"I do not know," said the man, "what the custom of the British may be. But it is the custom of the Irish to hate villains."

More Irish villagers began to show up. They were both curious and angry. When I tried to move away from them, one man tapped me on the shoulder and said, "Come, sir, you must follow me to Mr. Kirwin's, to explain yourself."

"Who is Mr. Kirwin? Why must I explain myself? Isn't Ireland a free country?"

"Yes, sir, free enough for honest folks. Mr. Kirwin is a judge, and you must explain the death of a gentleman who was found murdered here last night."

This answer startled me. I was innocent, and could easily prove it, but I followed him, and was led to a fancy house in town. I was very tired, but decided it was best to look awake, so as not to give anyone a bad impression.

I had no way of knowing the horror of what was about to happen.

Chapter 21

The judge seemed nice, but he looked at me harshly. He asked for witnesses, and six men came forward. The first said that the night before, he had found a man lying on the beach. He and his friends thought that the man might have drowned in the sea and washed up on shore, but his clothes were dry. Then they saw marks on his neck. I immediately thought of how my little brother had perished.

The man's son added that he had seen a boat out at sea, with a single man in it, just as I had been. He was sure it was the same boat. A woman claimed that where the body was discovered, she had seen a man push out to sea in a small boat. Others suggested that because the sea was rough, the man who left in the boat was not able to escape and had to return to the shore.

The judge asked that I be taken to where the man's body was, so they could see my reaction.

I went to the room where it was and was taken up to the coffin. How can I describe to you the horror of what I saw? There, lying in front of me was my dear friend, Henry Clerval! I cried out, "Have my actions killed you as well, my dearest Henry? I have already killed two others, but not you too!"

I fell to the floor and was carried out. A fever crept over me, and I was sick for two months, only half-awake and imagining all kinds of terrible things in my delirious illness. When I finally recovered, I was in a prison cell. At first, I didn't know why I was there, but soon it all came back to me.

An old woman sat next to me. "Are you better now, sir?" she asked.

"I believe I am," I said, "but if it's all true, then I am sorry to be alive!"

"If you're talking about the man you killed, then yes, things will be bad for you! I'm just here to see to it that you recover."

I think I still doubted if any of this was true.

One day the judge visited me.

"I hope that you will soon be set free," he said. "I believe that there is evidence to prove you are innocent. You floated to this shore by accident and were captured and charged with the murder of your friend, a murder that seems to have been committed by some other terrible fiend."

I was surprised that he seemed to know about me, and about how the monster must have done this.

"When you fell ill, I looked at the papers in your pockets, and found letters from Geneva. I wrote to your father. Someone is coming to visit you."

At first, I feared that the monster had come to mock me and torment me, and I told the judge that I didn't want to see anyone. But he told me that it was my father.

"My father?" I cried. "Where is he?"

No sooner had I said these words than he entered, and the judge left us alone. I reached out to him. "Are you safe? And Elizabeth?"

He told me that they were well, which made me feel better.

"What a terrible place to be in, my son," he said. "You traveled to be happy but have ended up in jail. And poor Henry is dead."

We talked for a short time, but I was still weak. My father being there made me feel much better, and my health began to improve. But the better I felt, the more I remembered what had happened.

Eventually, my case was brought before the judge, who was kind to me, after he had learned all about me. It was proven that I was still on the Orkney Islands in Scotland when the murder was committed, and I was soon free to go. My father was delighted that I was free, but for me, even being free didn't make me feel better. All I could think of was poor Henry, and the monster I'd set loose in the world.

I knew I had to do one thing: return to Switzerland, wait for the creature, and end his miserable existence once and for all. Soon we set sail from Ireland, and headed for home.

Chapter 22

We made it to Paris, where I found that I needed to rest before we could continue on our journey home to Geneva. But it was more than just my illness; my guilt weighed on me just as much, and I knew people would hate me if they learned what I had done.

Soon, I couldn't take it anymore. "Alas, my father!" I cried. "William, Justine, and Henry, they all died by my hands! It's my fault!"

"My son," he answered, "please never say that again!"

"I'm not crazy," I said. "It's my fault that they are gone. I would give anything to have saved them."

My father thought that I was ill again, so he changed the subject. He would not allow me to speak of it.

A few days before we left Paris on our way to Switzerland, I received a letter from Elizabeth:

My dear friend,

I am so glad that you are coming home! I heard that you were in jail, and I've been so worried. I don't wish to disturb you, but I feel that I must ask you something. Do you love me, truly? I know that our parents have long wanted us to be married, but if this is not what you wish, if you do not love me in that way, please be honest and tell me. I would never wish for you to be unhappy.

You don't need to answer right away. If you come back with a smile, I will know that all is well.

Elizabeth

This letter reminded me of what the monster had said: that he would be with me on my wedding night. And he would try to kill me, but I would have to make a stand and finish him. And then I would be free!

I knew that if I tried to put off our wedding, the monster might find some other way of having his revenge. So, I might as well go ahead with it, and face him, once and for all. I wrote back to Elizabeth and told her that I wanted nothing more than to marry her. I told her I had one terrible secret, which I would tell her the day after our wedding.

A week later, we returned to Switzerland. Elizabeth was so glad to see me that she cried.

Though I remembered again the words of the monster threatening me, I asked if the wedding could take place in ten days. If only I'd known what the creature really intended!

The wedding was planned, visitors came by, and I did the best I could to appear happy and carefree. Elizabeth had inherited a house in Italy, beside Lake Como. We agreed that we would go there for our honeymoon.

In the meantime, I made plans to defend myself. I carried weapons, and I was always watching to see if the monster would appear. This made me feel safer, and as the day approached, I began to think that maybe I had imagined it all, and it wouldn't happen.

On the day of the wedding, Elizabeth seemed a bit worried, as if she sensed something bad might happen, but I assured her that all was well. After the ceremony, we had a big party. Then we boarded a boat on the river bound for Italy that very night. Those were the last hours in my life of true happiness.

Chapter 23

We landed ashore after eight o'clock. It was getting dark, and a heavy rain fell on us.

I'd been calm and happy that day, but when night came, I was afraid and anxious again. Still, I knew I had to face the monster. Elizabeth saw that I was worried and asked me what was wrong. I assured her that it was just the night that scared me, and all would be well.

I asked her to go to bed, knowing that seeing me fight the creature would be upsetting.

She left me, and I walked around the house. I checked every corner, every place that my enemy might hide. I found no trace of him, and I began to hope that maybe he was not going to show up after all. Then I heard a dreadful scream, coming from the bedroom. My blood went cold,

and I hesitated for a moment. The scream came again, and I rushed into the room.

How I survived that moment, I do not know. She was there, lifeless on the bed, dead at the hands of that cruel monster. I fainted. When I recovered, I dashed to her, hoping that she might yet live, but I saw the marks of the monster's hands on her neck, and I knew she was gone.

In agony and sadness, I looked up. I saw in the open window the thing I most hated. The monster looked at me, and he grinned a terrible grin. I ran toward the window, but he leaped to the ground, and ran to the lake, plunging into it.

The noise attracted others, and I told them what had happened. I pointed to where the creature had disappeared, and they searched for several hours, but couldn't find him.

I tried to go with them, but I was too weak. My fever returned; I collapsed and was taken to a bed. Later, I came to and went to the room where Elizabeth lay. I realized that no one was safe from this creature, not my father, not my brother Ernest, no one. I had to go back to Switzerland as soon as possible.

Despite the rain, I returned home by the river. This fiend had taken all my happiness from me, and nothing could ever make me feel good again.

I arrived home. My father and brother Ernest were fine, but my father was devastated at the news about Elizabeth. It was so horrible that he was unable to get out of bed, and in a few days he died in my arms.

I went to the police and told them that I knew who was responsible for these deaths, and that I needed the help of the law to bring him to justice. I told them the truth about what I'd done. They didn't believe me at first, but as I continued, they became more interested, more horrified.

They told me that it would be very hard to capture him, and he would be almost impossible to find.

I said that I would devote my life to capturing the monster. I was more determined than ever to stop him, no matter how I had to do it.

Chapter 24

I decided to leave Switzerland forever. Before I left, I went to the cemetery, to the graves of William, Elizabeth, and my father. Sobbing, I vowed that I would live to get revenge on the monster and make him suffer as I had.

I was answered through the stillness of night by a loud and fiendish laugh. The mountains echoed it, and I felt as if the whole world mocked and laughed at me. The laughter died away, and a familiar voice whispered, "You have decided to live. I am satisfied, miserable man!" I ran to where I heard

the voice, but once again, the creature escaped from me. I caught sight of him in the moonlight, moving far faster than any human could. I chased after him, but lost him, as I have done so many times since then.

I was never able to catch up with him. In my sleep, I remembered Elizabeth, Henry, and my father, and missed them even more when I woke up.

I pursued him, and for many months this has been my task. Guided by a slight clue, I followed the windings of the Rhone River, but he was always too fast for me. I came to the blue Mediterranean Sea, and there, in the middle of the night, I saw the monster sneak onto a ship bound for the Black Sea. I boarded the same ship, but he escaped me somehow. Through the wilds of Russia, I followed his tracks. Sometimes the villagers, scared by his horrid face, told me which way he was going. Sometimes he himself, who feared that if I lost all trace of him I should despair and die, left some mark to guide me carved in tree bark or stone: "My reign is not yet over." Another said, "Follow me, I am going north. We may yet meet there."

And so, I began to journey north. I found another message: "Prepare yourself! Your struggle is only beginning. Soon, we will make a journey that will satisfy my hatred of you."

His taunts made me more determined not to fail. I bought a sled and snow dogs and traveled the land with great speed. I came to a small village by a northern ocean frozen over with ice, and I heard that the monster had been there only the day before. He took their food and dogs, and sped off in a sled, across the frozen sea. He was headed in a direction that led to no land; and the villagers thought that he would speedily be destroyed by the breaking of the ice or frozen by the eternal frosts.

But I knew his superhuman powers would keep him alive. I followed him, and even though getting across the icy sea was difficult, I didn't give up. I must have spent three weeks out there, when finally I saw a dark speck in the distance. It was him! I was so relieved that I cried.

After another two days, I was even closer! Then, the worst thing possible happened. Some of the ice in front of me began to crack, and before I could make it across, it fell into the water, leaving many waves in the between me and my enemy. Even worse, I was stuck on a drifting iceberg, and I knew that it was over.

Many hours passed, and I was freezing to death when I saw your ship in the distance. I was happy to learn that your boat was sailing north, so that I might still catch him.

Oh, must I perish, while he lives on? If this happens, Walton, swear to me that he will not escape, that you will seek him out and destroy him!

Arctic explorer and adventurer Robert Walton continues the story . . .

You've read this strange and terrible tale. Does it not horrify you and make your blood run cold?

I saw Frankenstein's monster myself! I wanted to know how he actually created it. "Are you crazy, my friend?" he said. "Would you make your own misery? Learn from my mistakes!"

The only comfort Frankenstein has is in his dreams where his friends and family are still with him. He thanked me for my kindness and said that the only goal he has left in life is to destroy his creation.

Our ship is surrounded by mountains of ice, in danger of being crushed. So, we must go back to England. Frankenstein wanted us to leave him on a glacier. But he was very sick, and he realized that he had failed to destroy the monster he'd made. He died, sorry for what he'd done, but not able to undo it.

It is now midnight, and I heard something . . . what was it? I entered Frankenstein's cabin and saw a huge creature standing over his coffin. His face was hidden in his hands, and I heard him crying. When he heard me, he jumped to the window, but turned to look back at me. Never have I seen anything so horrible, so hideous. But I asked him to stay.

He paused and looked at his creator.

"This man is also my victim!" he cried. "Oh Frankenstein, I would ask you to forgive me, but you are gone!"

"If you had felt guilty before," I said, "he would still be alive."

"Do you think I cannot feel guilty?" he answered. "His suffering was nothing compared to mine! I know I was selfish, but I regret everything. Do you think I enjoyed hurting people? I was made for love and friendship, but no one loved me. I am tortured by guilt that you cannot even imagine."

At first, I felt sorry for him, but I remembered that Frankenstein had told me this monster was persuasive.

"Fiend!" I said. "It is only because he is gone that you say these things. You do not feel pity; you regret it only because he is no longer here for you to torment!"

"That is not true," he answered. "But I know I will never find anyone who feels sorry for me. Once, I hoped that I would meet people who could see beyond my monstrous appearance and know the real being inside. But I am truly alone.

"You have only heard Frankenstein's version of the story. The truth is that my misery is beyond what you can imagine! You may hate me, but not as much as I hate myself.

"Do not fear that I will hurt you, or anyone else. My work is almost done. The only one left to finish is me! I will go to the North Pole on an iceberg. I will no longer feel pain or sadness, and I will have my rest.

"Farewell! You are the last person I will ever see. Frankenstein, if you still lived, you could not hope for greater revenge against me than I wish against myself.

"Soon, I will be gone, and my spirit will sleep in peace."

As he said this, he jumped from the cabin window down to the iceberg next to the ship. Then he drifted away on the waves, and he was lost in the darkness and distance.

THE END

About the Author

Mary Wollstonecraft Shelley was an English novelist. She was eighteen years old when she penned *Frankenstein; or, The Modern Prometheus*, which was first published in 1818. It is now considered one of the first pieces of science fiction or gothic literature, and one of the best horror stories of all time. Shelley also authored several other novels and edited the works of her husband, the Romantic poet Percy Bysshe Shelley.

In 1797, Shelley was born Mary Wollstonecraft Godwin in London, England. She was the daughter of Mary Wollstonecraft, author of *A Vindication of the Rights of Woman* (1792), and philosopher William Godwin. Her mother died soon after she was born, so Mary and her half-sister Fanny were raised by their father and stepmother. Mary could often be found visiting her mother's grave and reading and writing there. She once said, "As a child, I scribbled; and my favorite pastime, during the hours given me for recreation, was to 'write stories.'"

About the Editor

Margaret McGuire Novak is an editor and the author of several books. After completing her studies at Kenyon College, she found herself quickly swept up into the world of publishing. She lives with her family in Charlottesville, Virginia. Find her at margaretnovak.com.

About the Illustrator

Maïté Schmitt was born in a little town near Strasbourg in France, close to the German border. Her love of old animation movies inspired her to study illustration and animation. She has illustrated numerous books and worked on a short film, *A priori,* which combines two of her favorite things: books and bats. Say hello at maiteschmitt.com.

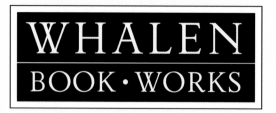

Whalen Book Works is a small, independent book publishing company based in Kennebunkport, Maine, that combines top-notch design, unique formats, and fresh content to create truly innovative gift books.

Our unconventional approach to bookmaking is a close-knit, creative, and collaborative process among authors, artists, designers, editors, and booksellers. We publish a small, carefully curated list each season, and we take the time to make each book exactly what it needs to be.

We believe in giving back. That's why we plant one tree for every ten books we sell. Your purchase supports a tree in a United States National Park. ♠

Get in touch!

Visit us at Whalenbooks.com or write to us at
68 North Street, Kennebunkport, ME 04046.